TALES FROM DOVER CASTLE

F.J. BEERLING

ILLUSTRATED BY GARETH BOWLER

Colin

Digger   Fletch   Alfie

Fairyfaye Publications
ISBN: 9780992826963

TALES FROM DOVER CASTLE

First paperback edition.

ISBN: 9780992826963

Published by Fairyfaye Publications
For events and all enquiries email fairyfayepublications@gmail.com

Edited by Denise Smith www.dspublishingservices.co.uk

www.fairyfayepublications.co.uk

Designed & set by Gareth Bowler

Printed in Great Britain

To English Heritage, thank you for bringing history to life.

F.B

For Nana.

G.B

**Special thanks to Julian Jennings without whom this book
would not have been possible.**

To my two lovely grandsons, Theo and Oliver.

J.J

Once upon a time, a pair of greedy rats
Flew down on a balloon to feast on snacks.

But the bins were empty now summer was over
At this medieval home on the cliffs of Dover.

They flew to a castle that looked out to sea,
Where Alfie and Fletch were hoping for tea.

So they hatched a plan to get them inside,
As luck was about to take them for a ride.

A lady with her shopping stopped by the bin,
Her bags full of food, so the pair dived in.

They fell amongst books, cookies and a bun,
And so their historic adventure had begun...

It began with a tour of the Castle, on wheels,
In a bag, on her scooter being driven up hills.

Then around the grounds and its 36 towers,
With tales of ghosts and kings of great powers.

Alfie was interested in the red history book,
So he put on some glasses and took a look.

"A Guide to Dover Castle," he read out loud,
Fletch whistled and clapped; Alfie felt proud.

So Alfie continued to read...

"Built between 1180 and 1185,
This medieval fortress really came alive,

"When King Henry II built the Great Tower
To show off his wealth and status and power."

As Fletch listened to Alfie, he started to scoff,
The scooter slowed down and the lady got off.

So Alfie poked a hole in the side of the bag,
And saw a huge tower with lions on a flag.

This was the great tower at 26 metres high,
30 metres square, flags flapping in the sky.

And with some of its walls 6.4 metres thick,
Breaking into this castle wouldn't be quick!

The excited little rats were carried inside
In a bag filled with food, their perfect ride.

Up a spiral staircase and
straight to the top,
As Fletch finished his bun,
boy, did he pop!

Then all of a sudden the carrier bag split.
They fell to the floor with nowhere to sit.

A chicken drumstick rolled under the bed,
So Alfie gave chase with a book on his head.

The lady reached down, her hand like a claw,
Grabbing at wrappers and books from the floor.

Quite unaware that her free-loading guests
Had eaten her food and, in fact, were pests!

They scoffed the chicken and fell asleep
In the Great Chamber at the top of a keep,

Quite unaware of their adventures ahead,
As they popped and snored on a King's bed.

They woke with bellies round and fat,
Slid down the bedding and fell on a mat.

Saw furniture painted in red, gold and blue,
And from their window a spectacular view.

The king had a chest, a wardrobe and chair,
A table with a chess set and window for air.

With curtains all around the huge painted bed,
And padded pillows for a king's weary head.

A feathered mattress and rug on the floor,
Even a toilet in the small room next door.

Tapestry rich hangings hung from the wall,
And breakfast, it was served in the great hall.

Inside the great hall there were tables galore,
More hangings on walls and a wooden floor

Where court was held and banquets took place,
As guests sat on benches and stuffed their face.

Alfie and Fletch were hungry once more,
So they left the great hall and went to explore.

Down the spiral staircase they made their way,
Exploring Dover Castle had taken all day!

The walls were cold, and old, and damp,
And the ceilings were ever so high.

There was no gas or central heating,
Or warm places for washing to dry.

In the guest bedroom were lots of beds,
With bedding and pillows for weary heads.

An open fireplace with a rug on the floor,
And even a curtain in place of the door.

But Alfie and Fletch were not amused,
They looked around but still no food.

So back down the spiral staircase they went,
It was made of stone and glued with cement.

They kept on going and did not stop,
Poor Fletch was nervous, he started to pop.

So Alfie ran faster to escape the smell,
Perhaps Fletch's tummy was not very well!

Finally they stopped going down and round,
And in the basement some food they found.

Great chunks of meat
hung from the ceiling,
They licked their lips,
a sight most appealing.

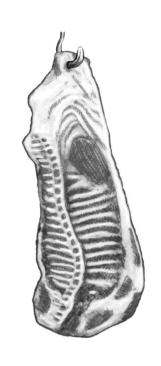

So Alfie stood up on
Fletch's shoulders,
Upon a small crate
and several boulders

But were still unable
to reach the food;
They were very hungry
and in a bad mood.

Locked in the castle
they started to shout:
"Help, we're trapped,
come and let us out!"

And as if by magic
a small mole appeared,
In a tin hat, with a torch
and mud for a beard!

"**H**ello, I'm Digger and I am a Mole.
Come back with me down this small hole."

So under the ground they followed Digger,
Until the light in the tunnel grew bigger.

They came to a hospital full of beds,
Where injured soldiers lay their heads.

Nursed back to health during WW2,
In this very tunnel from 1941 to 1942.

They kept on going and did not stop.
Cried Alfie to Digger: "Are we near the top?"

"No," replied Digger, "keep following me.
There's something else I want you to see."

Very soon they arrived and looked around,
In a top secret HQ deep under the ground.

Operation Dynamo was secretly planned
In this operations room, heavily manned.

On May the 26th and stranded in France,
French and British allies, but not by chance.

They were across the channel and out of reach,
So were told to wait upon Dunkirk beach.

Day and night for nine long days,
Admiral Ramsay masterminded ways

To safely rescue 338,000 troops,
And on 4th June evacuated them in groups.

As Alfie wiped a tear from his eye,
Closer they burrowed towards the sky.

Before very long they were back outside,
Where they left their birthday balloon ride.

Back in their bucket they flew over Dover,
Their magical history tour was now over.

But knowing much more of this great tower,
A royal residence where the king had power.

The castle on the cliffs is the place to go,
Step back in time, your knowledge will grow.

Explore great chamber's where a king once slept,
And underground tunnels where secrets were kept.

Alfie's Dover Castle Quiz

1. What is the front door of the Great Tower made from?

   A) Cream cheese   B) Wood   C) Plastic

2. What do you use to get to the upper floors of the Great Tower?

   A) A magic carpet   B) A spiral staircase   C) An elevator

3. What can you see on the tables inside the Great Hall?

   A) A pair of old boots   B) Chocolate biscuits   C) A silver dish/serving jug

4. What did guests sit on as they stuffed their faces?

   A) Comfy armchairs   B) Wooden benches   C) Whoopee cushions

5. Where does the King keep his clothes in the Great Chamber?

   A) In a heap on the floor   B) Under his pillow   C) In a wardrobe

6. What game can be seen on the table in the Great Chamber?

   A) A chess set   B) Naughts and crosses   C) Dominos

7. What was the name of the King who built Dover Castle?

   A) King Kong   B) King size bed   C) King Henry II

8. How many towers are there at Dover Castle?

   A) 1   B) 36   C) 100

9. The underground tunnels were also used during WW2 as what?

   A) A place to hang washing   B) A sweet shop   C) A hospital

10. Who took Alfie and Fletch on a tour of the underground tunnels?

   A) Father Christmas   B) Digger the Mole   C) Colin the Cockroach

We hope you enjoyed reading all about our adventures at Dover Castle, we had a great time, too!

Exploring a real castle and finding stuff out about it is so interesting and brilliant fun! In fact, Fletch had so much fun that it didn't all sink in!

Can you help him answer these questions in my Dover Castle quiz?

Answers....

1.B 2.B 3.C 4.B 5.C 6.A 7.C 8.B 9.C 10.B